DIARY OF A MINECRAFT ZOMBIE

BOOK 18

IN TOO DEEP

DIARY OF A MINECRAFT ZOMBIE

ZOMBIE

BOOK 18

IN TOO DEEP

BY
Zack Zombie

4

☀ SUNDAY ☀

YOU WANT ME TO DO WHAT?!!!

"Just jump in dude...It'll be fine."

"You do know Zombie's aren't supposed to get wet, right?!!

"Don't worry," Steve said. "The new potion I gave you will **TOTALLY** protect you."

I don't know how I get into these situations.

I guess Steve doesn't have any more villagers to practice his experiments on.

Actually, I think Steve's village officially labeled him a **"MENACE TO SOCIETY."**

I mean, I don't blame them. I think Steve's village has had more explosions than all the villages in the entire overworld combined.

"Dude, I'm telling you, it's going to be fine,"

"Are you sure?"

"Trust me," Steve said as he gave me his big eyes look.

I don't know why I trust this guy.

I mean, any reasonable Zombie would know better.

But for some reason I always end up in one of Steve's EXPERIMENTS.

And, I always end up with an extra arm, or a leg...

Or an extra mouth, where a mouth should never be.

So wrong.

"Alright I'll do it. Just don't rush me."

So, I decided to get in the lake.

First, I started by putting my toe in the water.

It felt really tingly.

Though, I think it was because all the maggots ran for cover.

Then I put my crooked ankle in the water...then my bony knee...then my...

"Just jump in dude!!!" Steve yelled as he **SHOVED** me in the water.

"AAAAAAAHHHHH!!!!"

SPLASH!

Glub...glub...glub!

This is it...this is the end!

I'm a goner for sure this time.

Goodbye cruel world!

Then I took a deep breath.

HOOOAAAAHHH!!!

But then I remembered... Hey, wait a minute. I'm a Zombie! I don't need to breathe.

Whoa! This is amazing!

I couldn't believe it.

There I was...under water, totally owning it.

Then Steve jumped in the water.
And it seemed like he didn't need to breathe either.

Wow, I guess that water breathing potion really did work.

Then Steve took a picture of me with his **UNDERWATER** camera.

Man, this is going to make the papers. The first Zombie to ever to go in water.

"Yo, check this out!" Steve said as he pulled the picture out of his camera.

Then Steve handed me the picture.

"Whoa, that's off the hook!"

"Look at you bro! You're like an underwater zombie!"

Wow, I can't wait to show this pic to all the kids at school.

I'm going to go down in **HISTORY** as the first underwater Zombie ever!

M✳NDAY

I brought my underwater picture to school today because I wanted show all my friends.

I knew they wouldn't believe that I **JUMPED** in the water and like, became the first underwater zombie.

Yeah, kids in school don't believe anything nowadays.

Like, one time I told my friends that I grew an extra head, and it gave me an identity crisis.

Of course, they totally didn't believe me.

Or, another time, I told them that a kid got me so mad once, that I ripped his head off, jumped down his throat and played with his heart.

Of course, they **DIDN'T BELIEVE** me.

They didn't even believe me when I told them that I traveled all the way to the moon because I was in the mood for some cheese.

Yeah, kids in school aren't as gullible as they used to be.

But this time, I had evidence.

They totally had to believe me now.

So when we got to math class, I started telling the guys about my underwater adventures.

Of course they didn't believe. That's because I was saving my underwater picture till later, so I can really show them who's **BOSS**.

But then, Ms. Bones interrupted us.

"Okay class take your seats. Today I have the results from your math quiz, and I have to say that I am very disappointed in some of you," Ms. Bones said looking right at me.

Or I think she was.

Mrs. Bones recently got laser eye surgery.

So now, Ms. Bones has **EYEBALLS**.

Except, I think the surgeon was cross-eyed, because both of her new eyeballs kind of stare in different directions.

She looks like a Chameleon...but without skin.

So now, I can't tell where she's looking half the time.

Makes it really hard to get away with stuff in class.

Adults...So weird.

Then Ms. Bones started to pass everybody's tests back to them.

But, when I got my test, it looked like the person who graded it had a nose bleed.

Oh man, that's a lot of red, I thought.

"Zombie, please speak to me after class," Ms. Bones said, looking **ANNOYED**...I think.

"Oooooohhhhh!" Everybody said.

I tried to act really cool, but I knew I was in trouble.

So I went over to speak to Mrs. Bones after class.

"Zombie, I'm sorry to say this, but unless you pick up your grades, you're going to fail this class," She said.

"Seriously?"

"Yes, and that will mean you will have to repeat **BEGINNERS MATH**, while all of your other friends will be in advanced math classes."

Oh man, I think I'm going to be sick.

"Zombie, you're so bright. Why aren't you doing better in class?"

"I don't know, Ms. Bones. I tried really hard to pass the test. But I just can't get math."

"I think you're just not applying yourself," Ms. Bones said, eyeing my underwater picture in my hand.

"Okay, Ms. Bones."

"If you would spend more time studying and less time engaged in all kinds of **SHENANIGANS**," She said grabbing my picture, "you would do so much better. So I will be taking this, thank you very much!"

"What?!!!!"

"The good news is that I am going to give another quiz on Thursday. So if you study hard and get an "A" that will help you do better and pass this class."

She calls that good news?

"Okay Zombie, now run along," Mrs. Bones said, while her eye balls darted back and forth.

Oh man, this is not good.

I'm going to have to study really hard to pass the next quiz.

But who am I kidding? Every time I try to study I can't concentrate long enough to remember anything.

Not to mention, my Zombie **PEA BRAIN** can only remember so much.

Then, when I walked out of class, a bunch of the kids ran up to me to see my underwater picture.

"No really! I did have it. Mrs. Bones just took it!"

"Yeah right man! What a poser! I knew you didn't jump underwater! You're so shady!"

Then they all walked away, as they trampled over my **DIGNITY** on the way out.

Man, not only am I going to fail math.

But, now all the kids in school think I'm a total poser.

Things couldn't get any worse.

TUESDAY

"Zombie, the reason I called you in today, is that I need to speak to you about your grades," the Creeper Principal said.

"Uh...Okay, Mr. Brown."

"Now, Ms. Bones told me that you **FAILED** your last math test. And you know Zombie, math is one of the most important subjects in school. And without passing math, you cannot pass to your next grade."

"Really?!!!!"

"Yes. So I am sorry to say this Zombie, but unless you pass Mrs. Bones' class, you're going to have to repeat a grade at school."

"What?!!!"

My stomach started to rumble. And I could feel my guts shifting around. Either that, or all the maggots were running for cover again.

"Uh...are you ok, Zombie?"

I felt like I was about to **EXPLODE.**

"I think so, Mr. Brown."

"And Zombie, I expect you to study really hard for this next quiz. And another thing..."

GRRRRRRRRR!

Principle Brown just gave me a weird look.

"So you'd better bring your grades up," He said, "or you'll flunk out of school, drop out of society and become a criminal... And then that means..."

SPLATTTTTTT!!!!

Then the Secretary ran into the Principal's office.

"Oh dear!" She said.

Then she tried to fish out Principal Brown.

GRRRRRRRRR!

SPLATTTTTT!!!!

Yeah, once I started, I couldn't stop.

GRRRRRRRRR!

SPLATTTTTT!!!!

Well, at least they now have a good reason to call it Principal Brown's office.

When I finally got home after school, I jumped into bed and crawled into a ball.

Then I started thinking about what Principal Brown said.

Oh man! I can't get left behind!

That'll like totally **DESTROY** any street cred I have at school.

Not to mention that all my friends are going to leave me behind!

And then they'll totally forget me... Sniff.

...And then I'll drop out of society... Sniff...And become a criminal...Sniff... and eventually fade out of existence... Sniff.

Or, worse!

I might end up like...

LARRY LARDBOTTOM!

Man, Larry got left back so many times, they made him the honorary janitor.

He didn't even have enough credits to work in the cafeteria.

Urrrggghhh! Why am I having so much trouble with math?!!!

I mean, it sorta makes sense, in a boring and confusing kind of way.

But then, when they put a **MATH TEST** in front of me, I like totally freeze and forget everything!

Oh man, what am I going to do?

WEDNESDAY

I decided to talk to Steve to see if he could help me **PASS** my next math exam.

Steve knows just about everything there is to know about everything.

Man, I'm sure he knows everything about math! I thought.

I found him at his favorite spot punching his tree.

"Hey Steve."

"Oh, hey Zombie. Wanna join me for a workout?" Steve said, kinda sweaty.

"Naw man, Zombie's can't sweat. So when we work out, we just end up smelling like pickles."

Steve just looked at me...confused.

"So Zombie, what's up?" Steve asked.

"Uh...hey are you any good at math?"

"Math? PFFFFFFFT! I'm **TERRIBLE** at math," Steve blurted

"What?!!!"

"Yeah, man. I'm so bad at math, I took my math book to the psychiatrist because the teacher said it had a lot of problems."

"Seriously?!!!"

"Yeah, man. Sorry. I was never really good at it. That's why I was really glad when they invented the **MATH APP** on my phone. Now whenever I have to do math, I just whip out my phone."

I just stood there confused.

"But...Um...Don't they say that if you don't know math, you're going to drop out of society and become a **CRIMINAL**, and eventually fade out of existence?"

"Uh...whose THEY?" Steve asked.

"Um...you know, THEM!"

"Who?"

"You know...THEM!"

Steve just shrugged his shoulders.

"Well, that's what all the teacher's at school say."

"I don't know man. Why don't you just use a math app to take your test at school. It should make it **REALLY EASY**. And you'll probably finish really quick."

"Dude, that's a great idea!"

"You're welcome," Steve said, and went back to punching his tree.

When I started walking away, a strange thought did cross my mind.

What if I don't learn math, and I spend the rest of my life punching trees?

It just felt shivers down my spine.

But man, that was like the **BEST IDEA** ever!

So, when I got home I downloaded the best math app I could find on my phone.

The name of the app was called, "Math for Dummies...Cheaters Edition."

I kinda took offense that it was calling me a **DUMMY**.

But if it could help me through my quiz tomorrow, I didn't even care!

Math exam, here I come!

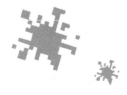

✳ THURSDAY ✳

Aced math exam today!

So easy.

Man, I'm going to totally ace the math final that's coming in a few weeks too.

Ahhhh! **LIFE IS SO GOOD**.

FRIDAY

"Mr. and Mrs. Zombie, thank you for coming in today," Principal Brown said. "The reason we had to call you to school today is that we believe that your son Zombie was **CHEATING**."

"GASP!!!!"

I had never seen my Mom and Dad turn **WHITE** before.

And it was really weird shade of white too.

Kinda like moldy cheese that was left on the porch on a hot summer day.

"There must be some mistake, Principal Brown," my Mom said. "We raised our son too well to do that."

"Yes, there must be some mistake," Dad said.

"Well, please brace yourselves, but we have **EVIDENCE**," Then Principal Brown took my exam out to show my parents.

"This test reveals that your son Zombie got every answer right, for a perfect score of an A+."

"GASP!!!!"

Wow, I was really offended by that response.

Then my parents looked at me.

"Son, how could you?" my Mom asked, before she started crying.

"It was really easy," I said. "I just used this math app on my phone. See, "Math for Dummies...Cheaters Edition."

"GASP!!!!"

"Yeah, it made the math test really easy. And it was a **LOT OF FUN**. I think I'm finally starting to get math now."

"GASP!!!!"

I really couldn't understand what the big deal was.

"Young man, you cannot use calculators or math apps when you take your test!" Principal Brown blurted.

"Why not? It made it really easy...and fun."

"Well....Uh...You just can't! You need to learn how to do it with **PENCIL AND PAPER** and work out all of the problems, and show all your work. That way you can understand all of the painstaking work that goes into it!" Principal Brown yelled.

"Zombie, how could you!" my Mom kept yelling in between sobs.

"Yes, son, how could you!" my Dad yelled also...in between sobs.

I was totally confused.

"I don't get it. If using a math app made math easy...and fun, why can't I use it?"

"YOU JUST CAN'T!!!" my Mom, Dad and Principle Brown yelled... in between sobs.

"Well, since this is Zombie's first offense, I am going to let him off with a warning," Principal Brown continued. "But Zombie, you have a math final exam in a few weeks. And if you don't pass that exam, I am sorry, but you are going to have to repeat a grade!"

"GASP!!!!"

"Zombie, how could you!" my Mom kept yelling in between sobs.

"Yes son, how could you!" my Dad yelled also...in between SOBS.

Man, I thought being a preteen was tough, but now, I'm totally confused.

I just stood there, totally feeling like I was going to be sick.

GRRRRRRRRR!

Right then, the secretary ran in.

"Is everyone okay? I thought I heard an animal?" She said.

GRRRRRRRRR!

SPLATTTTTT!

SATURDAY

I went to go see Steve again today.

"Dude, are you all right?" Steve asked. "You look a little shorter than usual."

"Yeah, I'm good. I just lost a little weight, that's all."

"Hey, since you're here, I got a joke for you," Steve said.

"Yeah, I could really use a **GOOD LAUGH** right now."

"Knock, Knock."

"Whose there?"

"I eat mop."

"I eat mop who?"

"Ewwwwww! Dude, you're nasty!"

"PFFFFFFTTTTT!"

Then we both burst out **LAUGHING**.

Man, I needed that.

"Dude, I need your help," I said. "I need to pass my math final that's coming in a few weeks, or I'm going to be left back in school!"

"What's so bad about that? Doesn't that mean you'll just have more time to learn stuff?"

"Naw man! That's gonna totally ruin my social life. And then I'm going to drop out of society, and become a criminal, and then I going to become a janitor at my school."

Steve just looked at me...Confused.

"Dude, I need your help....please!!!"

Then, I just broke down crying.

"WAAAAAAAAAHHHH!!!"

"Dude, I'll help you man! I promise!"

"Thanks...Sniff....man...Sniff."

"Actually, I can't help you, but I know who can," Steve said. "There's a full moon tomorrow, and that means

Glenda the Witch will be back in town. I'm sure she has some kind of potion that can make you smarter."

I was so happy, I started crying again.

"WAAAAAAAAHHHH!!!"

"Thank you, thank you, **THANK YOU!** Sniff...Sniff."

"Don't mention it bro."

GRRRRRRRRR!

Then I saw a strange look on Steve's face.

"Wow, you weren't kidding. You totally smell like pickles."

☀ SUNDAY ☀

So me and Steve went to go see
GLENDA THE WITCH in the
Swamp Biome today.

I kinda like the Swamp Biome.

It reminds me of my room.

All it needs is a nice booger collection,
and I could live here forever.

Anyway, we made it to Glenda's hut
and I kinda did a double take before I
went in.

"Hey, wait a minute. Didn't Glenda used to eat rotten flesh?"

"Oh yeah. But, you don't have to worry about that now. She said she's now a practicing **VEGETARIAN**."

"Great!"

"Except on Sundays."

"Wait...what?"

CRREEEEAAAAKKK!

"Zombie! Steve! I'm so happy you're here. You arrived just in time for **DINNER**." Glenda said.

"What was that now?" I said, trying to pull my sleeves down.

"Glenda, you look different," Steve said. "Did you do something to your hair?"

"Oh no, this is my **NEW BODY**," She said. "Do you like it?"

"Yeah sure," Steve said.

Though I think I was a bit weirded out that a 600-hundred-year-old Witch was kinda flirting with him.

"I'm just kidding," She said. "This body is just so that I don't **SCARE AWAY** my customers. They're not used to my human form you know."

Then Glenda zapped herself back to her usual self.

"Whoa! I always love when you do that." Steve said.

"Anyway, how can I help you boys?"

"Well, I have this math test that I have to take, and if I don't pass I'm going to be left back, and I am going to drop out of society, and I am going to become a criminal, and then I'm going to end up working at my school as a janitor, and...."

"Dude, breathe," Steve said.

"Yes, Zombie that was a mouthful. But it sounds like you want a potion to help make you SMARTER?"

"Yeah, that's it! I want to be smarter because my Zombie pea brain makes it really hard to study... and when I try to study I can't remember anything... and I need to pass my next math test that is in a few weeks... and if I don't pass I'll get left back... and then I will drop of out of society, and then I'll become a criminal, and then I'll work as a janitor...."

"Dude, **BREATHE**," Steve said.

"Oh...Sorry."

Then I looked over at Glenda and she looked like she was trying to remember something.

"Now where did I put that book? Hmmm."

Then she started rummaging through an old chest.

"Ah yes! Here it is!" She said, pulling out an old book that looked like it was made of...of...Rotten Zombie Flesh!"

"AAAAAAAAAHHHHH!!!!"

"Dude, what's the matter?!!!"

"Her book...it's made of Zombie flesh!...
ZOMBIE FLESH, man!"

"Oh, don't worry Zombie. No harm came
to any Zombies to make this book..."

"Whoooo, I was worried there for a
minute."

"At least not any that are still alive
to talk about it."

"Wait...what?"

"Dude you really need to calm down
man. Glenda is chill," Steve said.

Well, I couldn't argue with Steve, especially with his big eyeballs.

"Here it is!" Glenda said, after turning a few pages of the Zombie flesh book. "Zombie, it looks like what you need, is some **BRAIN CORAL!**"

"Brain Coral? What's that?"

"Well, brain coral is a special flower that grows underwater. It is said that if you drink a potion made from it, your brain will grow to a humongous size and it will give you all of the knowledge in the universe."

"Seriously?"

"Well, not really, that's just the legend. But I do know that brain coral potion will at least help you be smart enough to pass your math test," Glenda said.

"That's awesome! Where do we find it? Me and Steve can go out to get it right now!"

"Well, it says here that you can find it in...Oh no," Glenda said with a SURPRISED look on her face.

"What? What is it?"

"Well, it says here, that the only place to find it is in the Lost Ocean Temple of Atlantis."

"Oh man," Steve said.

"What? Where's the Lost Ocean Temple of Atlantis?"

"Well, Zombie that's the problem," Glenda said. "Nobody knows where it is. And anyone that has ever tried to find it, well...they've never come back."

Then Steve and I looked at each other.

"DUN...DUN... DUNNNNNNN!" We both said.

Then we burst out laughing.

"Why are you laughing?" Glenda asked.

"Well, me and Zombie eat danger for breakfast!" Steve said puffing out his big square chest.

"Yeah...We eat danger...for...uh...breakfast," I said, as my chest slowly deflated.

"Okay. Well, I do have a clue here," Glenda continued. "It says here, that the entrance to the Lost Ocean Temple of Atlantis can only be seen during the full moon. And the next full moon is not until...let me look at my calendar...Uh...**NEXT SUNDAY**."

"Wait! That's only a few days before my math final!"

But I could already see Steve getting more and more excited, the more dangerous and more challenging our adventure became.

"I hate you, you know that," I said to him.

Then he smiled and gave me a big **THUMBS UP**.

M✷NDAY

I tried to see if I could study today.

But no matter how hard I tried, I kept falling asleep.

And for some reason, every time I woke up, there was a game CONTROLLER in my hand.

Urrrgghhh! Why does studying make me so sleepy?

I mean like, I had all this energy after playing about twenty levels of my favorite videogame.

And, as soon as I start studying, I get really sleepy.

Like, I even get sleepy thinking about studying...

ZZZZZZZZZ!

"Zombie! You fell **ASLEEP** again!" my Mom yelled.

"Urrrgghhwuzzzat?"

See what I mean?

I even tried keeping my eye sockets open with some paper clips.

Except the paperclips just kept falling into my head and shooting out my nose cavity.

I kinda made a game of it, actually.

I tried to see how long I could make the snot trail as I blew the paperclip out of my nose.

Seriously, I almost got it to about three feet.

It was awesome.

Except my room is now covered in a giant **SNOT WEB**.

So cool.

What am I doing?!!!

I need to get back to studying.

Okay, here we go.

"A train leaves the Forest Biome traveling at 60 miles per hour, and a car leaves the Desert Biome traveling at 53 miles per hour. The train and car cross each other in the Swamp Biome. So what is the distance...

ZZZZZZZ...°

ZZZZZZZZZ!!!

ZZZZZZZZZ!!!

"Zombie! You fell asleep again!" my Mom yelled.

"Urrrgghhwuzzzat?"

Aww man, I got the game controller in my hand again.

And why do I have tire marks on my face?

Whatever, I need to get serious.

Math! Let's do this!

BUDABLING!

Yeah! I got a message on **SNAPBRAT.**

Awww that's so cute.

Ewww, that's gross.

Ha! It's a Meme about how kids get distracted from studying because they spend so much time on SnapBrat.

So funny.

Oh man, what am I doing? I need to get back to **STUDYING!**

Now where was I?

Math....Okay...A plane leaves the Forest Biome...

RRRRIIIIIIINNNNNNGGGG!!!

"Oh, hey Steve, what's happening?"

"No, not much. I'm trying to study for this math final."

"What do you mean, stand on my head? How's that going to help?"

"What does rubbing my belly supposed to do?"

"Are you just making that up?"

Seriously? Okay, I guess I can try it."

"Alright, I'll talk to you later man."

CLICK.

Well, here goes nothing.

It's a good think that I have a
SQUARE HEAD.

"Okay, a plane leaves the Forest Biome traveling at...ZZZZZZZZ!"

ZZZZZZZZ!!!

RRRRIIIIIINNNNNGGGG!!!

"Urrrggghhhwhat?"

"Oh, Hey Steve. Whatcha doing man?"

"Did what work?"

"Standing on my head? What's that for?"

"Oh, it's supposed to help me with my **MEMORY**? Yeah, I can try it."

"Rub my tummy? Are you sure? Okay man, I guess I can try it. I'll talk to you later."

Well, I'd better get back to studying.

Hmmm....I wonder what time it is.

WHAT?!!!!

It's like almost time for **SCHOOL**!

Urrrrghhh!, I hate Minecraft time!

TUESDAY

Well today we went on a field trip to the MINECRAFT AQUARIUM.

It was really cool.

Like, I like the Aquarium because it's got all kinds of creatures from the ocean.

Things like squid, and turtles, and dolphins...and they even have a shark!

Yeah, sharks are like the total bomb.

Except I was really looking forward to seeing the six-headed ones.

Those are really awesome.

But they didn't have any.

But they did have a really cool **SHARKNADO** exhibit that was totally off the hook.

"Hey Zombie, check this out," Skelly said, making funny faces at the giant shark in the big tank.

BLEEEHHH!

"Dude, are you sure you should be doing that?" I asked him.

"Yeah, he can't do anything. He's totally locked up in the tank," Skelly said.

BLEEEHHH!

Skelly just kept making faces at the shark.

Thump! Thump! Thump!

Then the shark started **BANGING** its head against the glass.

"Dude, you should really stop that," I said. "I don't think it's safe."

"It's totally safe," Skelly said. "This is like really thick glass."

BLEEEHHH!

Why do I get this feeling something REALLY BAD is about to happen?

"Okay kids. Gather around," Ms. Bones said, looking at the floor and ceiling at the same time.

All the kids gathered around in front of the giant fish tank that surrounded the whole room.

Except for Skelly, he stayed behind to make fun at the shark.

BLEEEHHH!

"This is Ms. Calamari," Mrs. Bones said. "She's going to tell us more about the wonderful world of underwater life."

"Cool!"

"Well, kids, there is a beautiful underwater world out there that has all types of animals, plants and **UNDERWATER MOBS**."

"Whoa!"

"Yes, some animals are friendly, like squid, turtles and dolphins."

"Whoa!"

"But some animals are very dangerous, like **MOB-EATING** sharks."

"Whoa!"

"Yes, there are different sizes of Mob-eating sharks too. There are sharks as small as my hand, and there are sharks that are as big as a house!"

"Whoa!"

Then one of the Creeper kids raised his hand.

"Yes, Cory?" Ms. Calamari said.

"Excuse me, Ms. Calamari. Do you have any Mob-eating sharks at this aquarium?"

HSSSSSSSS.

Yeah, I could tell Cory was getting scared.

And some of the other kids were getting scared to.

"Why, yes, we do, Cory. We have one of the **BIGGEST** Mob-eating sharks ever caught. But don't worry, you're totally safe. But whatever you do, don't make fun of him during his feeding time."

Then all of a sudden, the giant shark swam by the tank behind Ms. Calamari.

AAAAAAAAHHHHHH!!!!!

Then the kids started yelling and screaming.

HSSSSSSSS.

...And hissing.

"Don't worry, you're all safe. You can calm down now."

Then we saw the Mob-eating shark chasing Skelly through the tank!

AAAAAAAAHHHHHH!!!!!

"Oh dear! How did he get in there!" Ms. Calamari said.

"Alright kids, everybody out!" Ms. Bones said.

And then we all ran out of the aquarium, while they called the attendants to try to help Skelly.

When we all got out, Ms. Bones did a head count.

"Hey, where's Cory?" One of the kids said.

BBOOOOOOMMMM!!!!!!

Uh, something tells me Cory the Creeper didn't make it out.

WEDNESDAY

Well, I know what you're probably thinking.

But actually, Skelly is totally alright.

But man, we owe a serious shout out to Cory the Creeper.

He totally saved the day.

That kid like, deserves a **MEDAL**.

...And a moment of **SILENCE**.

✳ THURSDAY ✳

Well, it's going to be a few days until me and Steve risk life and limb to get to the Lost Ocean Temple of Atlantis.

So, I decided to take my mind off things and try to be a **REGULAR** Zombie for once.

So, I decided to practice a little on my skateboard.

You don't need a lot of brains to skateboard, so it was perfect.

"Hey Mom! Where's my skateboard?!!!" I yelled downstairs.

"I don't know! Did you check the garage?"

Urgghhh! Its probably all dirty and stuff.

Ewwww. And it's probably got spider webs too, yuck!

So I went into the garage and got my **SKATEBOARD**.

"Zombie, whatcha doing?" my little brother Wesley asked me, as he walked into the kitchen riding his chicken.

"I'm going to skateboard to school," I said.

"Why?" Wesley asked me.

"Because it's **COOL**."

"Why is it cool?"

"Because...I don't know, it's just cool!" I said annoyed.

"Why is it dirty?"

"Because it was in the garage. I just need to get a rag to clean it, so don't touch my skateboard, Okay!"

"Otay."

After a few minutes, I found a rag, a bucket and some soap. Then, I went back to the kitchen to get my skateboard.

But, when I got there it was all wet, and totally **CLEAN**.

"Hey, did you clean my skateboard?" I asked Wesley.

"Ummm, hmmm." Wesley said, looking really **SCARED**.

"Oh, thanks little bro," I said trying to let him know how much I appreciated it.

I mean, it was really nice of him.

Then he smiled, and happily went on his way.

Wow, that was really nice of Wesley.

Even though he has become more of a pain the older he gets.

It's like, now that he's older, he's always asking questions.

Like, he keeps **ASKING** me why I do everything.

"Zombie, why are wearing your hair like that?"

"Zombie, why are you always crying?"

"Zombie, why do you spend so long in the bathroom?"

"Zombie, what happens if your phone falls in the potty?"

It really gets annoying after a while.

And like, the older he gets, the weirder he gets.

Like, the other day, my Mom asked him why his toy dinosaurs were all wet.

And he said he PEED on them because they were thirsty.

Or the other day, my Mom asked him why his chicken was wet.

And Wesley said he peed on him to make him look pretty.

Anyway, it was really nice of him to clean my skateboard.

Wait...

FRIDAY

So all day yesterday people were looking at me and holding their noses.

Yeah, **ZOMBIE PEE** is not the nicest smell in the world.

Kinda smells like a somebody took toe jam, pee and brussel sprouts, blended them together, and left it outside in the sun to grow fungus...for a few years.

"Hey, Zombie," Skelly said, "You smell better today."

"Yeah, whatever..."

Then Heather Huskly came by our table in the cafeteria.

"Hey Zombie," she said in her usual deep voice.

"Hey Heather," I said, trying not to look directly into her **EYE SOCKETS**.

If you didn't know, Heather Huskly and her family just moved into town last month.

And she's only been here a month, and she's like, one of the most popular girls in school.

I think it's because people aren't used to seeing a husk family.

They're kind of a little different than regular Zombies.

"Hey Zombie, I'm having my birthday party tomorrow, and I wanted to **INVITE** you to come, if you would like."

"A party! Hey count me in," Skelly said.

"You can count me in too," Slimey said, walking up to us.

"Me too," Creepy said sneaking up on us too.

"Yeah, you're all welcome to come," Heather said. "We're going to have a pool party this year, so its going to be really awesome."

Then she wrote her address on my notebook and walked away.

"Woooooo, Zombie's got a new **GIRLFRIEND**!" the other guys said.

"No I don't!" I said embarrassed.

But you know, Heather was kinda pretty, in a girl with a manly voice kind of way.

"Uh...guys, did she say pool party?" Slimey said.

"Yeah, I love the pool!" Creepy said.

Then Creepy noticed Slimey's sad face.

"Oh, sorry Slimey, I totally forgot."

We all looked at Slimey who had a really **LONG FACE**...Well, longer than usual, I mean.

Yeah, Slimey is still really scared of the water.

He told me it was because when he was a kid, he tried to swim once, and he just sank right to the bottom.

Not to mention we had a sleepover at my house one time, and we saw Six Headed Shark Attack part one, two, three and four...and five.

Man, that movie totally made me afraid of the water for weeks.

So I can totally understand why Slimey's scared of the water.

"Guess we need to cancel," Skelly said.

"Hey, wait a minute! Steve just came up with the coolest **POTION** that helps mobs breathe underwater!" I said. "It's called the water-breathing potion."

"Yeah, we heard that one before," Skelly said rolling his eyes.

"No, its for real. I'm serious. I was like underwater for like ten minutes."

"Are you pulling our chain?" Skelly asked.

"Naw, I'm serious. It felt really weird...and tingly."

"Great, then let's do it!" Slimey said really happy.

So, we're all going to the coolest **POOL PARTY** of the year.

And who knows, maybe me and Heather can really get to know each other at her party.

But I don't know.

Maybe Heather and I wouldn't make a good couple.

I mean, she's cute and all.

But I'm not sure if I could get used to her manly voice.

...Or her mustache.

* SATURDAY *

All the guys were going to meet me outside Heather's house, so we could all come in like an ENTOURAGE.

"Dude, what's the fishing pole for?" I asked Skelly.

"I don't know. I've never been to a pool party before," He said. "How about you? What's up with the furry animals?"

"Those are my armpits, man!" I said, starting to feel self-conscious about having my shirt off.

"Hey Zombie, do you have the potion?" Slimey asked me.

"Sure do...Here you go," I said handing him a **PLASTIC CUP**.

I poured some for him, but I decided to save some for me for later.

"Bottoms up, man," I said as he took a swig.

"Ooooo, I feel tingly," Slimey said.

"Really?" Creepy asked.

"Yeah, I feel awesome!" Slimey said. "Let's do dis!"

Then Slimey put on his shades and started struttin' like a boss.

When we got to Heather's house, it was humongous.

Man, being a husk has some serious perks.

Then Slimey went to the bathroom to put his SWIM TRUNKS on.

Yeah, Slimey's trunks double as a piano cover, so he needs like 10 minutes to put them on.

So the rest of us walked over to the backyard, and it was also huge.

And there must've been like 100 mob kids out there.

"Whoa!"

Except, for some reason, nobody was going into the pool.

Then, when Slimey finally made it to the back yard, he just stood there with his mouth open.

"Oh my gosh, Zombie, this is awesome!" Slimey said.

I guess Slimey had dreams about finally being **INVITED** to a pool party one day.

He couldn't stop drooling at the sight of that big pool.

I didn't see what the big deal was, but hey, let the kid have his day.

"Do your thing, brah," I said.

But, I think I spoke too soon.

All of sudden, Slimey backed up about like ten feet, and then...

"HIIIYYAAAAAHHHH!!!!"

BWWWOOOOSSSSSHHHHH!!!!!

The water must've shot up about 50 feet in the air.

We all got **SOAKED**.

Then, it got quiet for a few seconds.

Then suddenly, next thing you know, all the kids started yelling and screaming and jumping in the pool.

"WOOOO-HHOOOOOO!!!!!"

BWWWOOOOSSSSSHHHHH!!!!!

Yeah, the party really got going after that.

I decided to go to bathroom to see if I could comb down my ARMPITS.

The water was getting them a bit frizzy...and curly.

"Hi Zombie, thanks for making it to my party," Heather said.

"Oh, yeah, thanks for inviting me," I said, trying not to move my arms.

"Wow, your friend Slimey is really having a great time," Heather said. "If he keeps belly flopping, there won't be any water left in the pool."

"Yeah, Slimey likes to really let loose, he...he..."

RRRRINNNNNGGG!

Then my cell phone rang.

"Uh, Heather, can you give me a minute," I said, trying to get to my phone without moving my arms.

I walked as fast as I could to the bathroom and closed the door nice and tight.

RRRRINNNNNGGG!

Steve? I wonder what he calling for?

"Whaddup Steve? Man, you should see Slimey. That potion you gave me is like making him totally crazy about belly flopping in the pool," I said.

MRRRMMMRRRR....

"Wait...what? I can't hear you."

Then Steve got louder, "I said...I gave you the wrong potion! I gave you a potion of **BRAVERY**, not the potion for water-breathing!"

"WHAT?!!!!!!"

"Yeah, man. Sorry about that. I forgot to put the labels on and..."

Perclunk!

"Aw man! I dropped my phone in the toilet!"

Urgghh!!! Now I had to fish my phone
out of the bowl.

It's a good thing my phone was
WATERPROOF.

And it's good the toilet was empty.

Except for a few tootsie rolls in there.

So weird.

Then I ran out to tell Slimey what
Steve said.

Next thing I know, all the kids were
cheering.

SLIMEY! SLIMEY! SLIMEY!

When I looked up, slimey was on a
really high diving board.

I tried waving my arms, but I started getting really weird looks.

So I started waving my hands instead.

But it was no use, Slimey couldn't hear me.

And before I knew it, Slimey started **BOUNCING**.

BOING! BOING! BOING!

Then Slimey jumped up 20 feet in the air...

"WWHHHOOOAAAA!!!!!"

And he came down with the ultimate belly flop.

BWWWOOOOSSSSSHHHHH!!!!!

Everything was quiet for a few seconds.

Then...

YYYYYEEEAAAAAAAHHHHH!!!!!

Everybody started **YELLING** and screaming their heads off.

YYYYYEEEAAAAAAAHHHHH!!!!!

Slimey climbed out the pool and took a bow.

"Oh hey, Zombie. Did you see my dismount?" Slimey said.

"Yeah, man. It was **AWESOME**."

"Hey what were you waving at me for?"

"Oh nothing.... Nothing."

"Cool, well I'm going back in!" Slimey said as he got back in line to the **DIVING BOARD**.

BWWWOOOOSSSSSHHHHH!!!!!

After seeing all the fun Slimey was having, I didn't have the heart to tell him what Steve said.

So I took out the bravery potion and took a swig of it myself.

But there wasn't much left.

So I was only brave enough to get in the kiddie side of the pool.

But it wasn't that bad, I guess.

I mean, the water was a bit warmer than the rest of the pool.

And there was the occasional orange **CREAM CHEESE** that floated by.

But besides that, it was okay.

Though, I still didn't get what all the floating tootsie rolls were for.

Wait...

SATURDAY,
LATER THAT NIGHT...

I tried to enjoy myself at the party.

I mean, I started having fun.

That was until I started thinking about my **MATH FINAL** next week.

And then all my fun went down the drain.

So, when I got home I tried to study, but I fell asleep again.

And when I woke up, not only did I have a game console in my hand, but

I also had the TV remote in my other hand, I was sleeping on some comic books, and I had a box of pizza for a pillow.

Yeah, I might as well give up.

But, you know, even though the test is only a few days away...You know what? I'm not going to worry.

Because there's still **HOPE**.

Me and Steve are going to go find the Brain Coral tomorrow, and it's going to make me so smart I'm going to ace that math final exam in like five minutes.

Man, I won't even need to go to school because I'll be so smart.

Yeah, life is going to be so easy from now on.....YAWN!

Yeah..So easy.....

* SUNDAY *

Well, today's the day.

"Today's the day me and Steve are going to go diving to go find the **LOST OCEAN TEMPLE OF ATLANTIS**."

Oh man.

Now that I just said that out loud, I'm not so sure I want to do this.

DING DONG!

"Zombie! Steve is here for you," my Mom yelled from downstairs.

"Okay Mom!"

Well, Steve is here, so there's no backing out now.

Knock, Knock!

"Come in!"

"Oh hey dude...
Whoa! What are
you **WEARING**?"

"AAARRGGHH!"
Steve said, acting
all weird and pushing out his chest
through his ruffled shirt.

"Uh...Urrrggghh!"

"AAARRGGHH!"

Urrrggghh!"

"AAARRGGHH!"

"Dude, I know you're trying to tell me something, but I just don't get it."

"Naw man, I was trying out my PIRATE VOICE, AAARRGGHH!"

"Ooookay. Uh, Steve, I think you've been drinking like too many potions, dude."

"Ha! I'm just ready for our next great adventure! AAARRGGHH!"

"Okay then. But speaking of potions, did you bring the right one this time?"

"Yup, here it is. The best water breathing potion there is."

"Seriously?"

"Yeah, normally it only last for about ten minutes. But I got Glenda to put a spell on it to last a really long time."

"Sweet."

So, I packed all of my stuff, and me and Steve walked down to the lake.

"Whoa! What is that?!!!"

"That's my **SHIP**. Do you like it?"

"Seriously? I didn't even know you had a ship."

"Yeah, I just built it last night. I thought if we were going on and adventure, we might as well go in style."

Man, I guess punching trees really does come in **HANDY**.

Get it...handy...tee, hee.

"So, let's set sail, and start our epic adventure, AAARRGGHH!"

"Yeah, whatever."

Well, we're about to embark on the most dangerous adventure yet.

But if it helps me pass my math final, it's going to be so worth it.

Man, I just hope my bladder holds up.

That's when I noticed something.

"Hey dude. Where are the bathrooms?"

Then Steve just smiled and pointed at the **HORIZON**.

Figures.

SUNDAY,
LATER...

We sailed for a little while until we got to a giant rock in the middle of the ocean.

"Well, I think this is the place," Steve said. "Glenda said when we find the giant rock in the middle of the ocean, then we'd be right over the **ENTRANCE** to the Lost Ocean Temple of Atlantis."

The big full moon was shining down and made the rock look like a face.

Kinda looked a little like Skelly, actually.

"Well dude, this is it," Steve said. "You ready?"

"Gulp! Uh...As ready as I'll ever be."

Then Steve pulled out his sparkly potion bottle.

"BOTTOMS UP DUDE," He said, taking a swig.

Then he passed it to me, and I took a swig.

Gulp!

Suddenly, I started getting that weird feeling again.

"Ooooh, I feel so tingly," I said trying not to fall down.

"SPLOOOSH!"

Next thing I know, Steve jumped in the ocean.

"Come on in, the water's fine!"

Well, here goes **NOTHING**!"

"SPLOOOSH!"

☀ SUNDAY, ☀
EVEN LATER...

"Whoa! This place is **AMAZING**!"

This was the first time I had ever seen the ocean, and I couldn't believe how awesome it was!

"Dude, is this sick or what?"

"It's got colors I've never even seen before!"

So sick.

We were swimming for a while, when off in the distance we saw a huge **UNDERWATER SHIP**.

"Dude, what's a ship doing down here?" I asked Steve.

"I don't know...Let's go check it out!"

How did I know he was going to say that?

So, we swam up to the ship and it had the weirdest **FLAG** on it.

Kinda looked like Skelly, but with a dull, lifeless expression...On second thought, it looked exactly like Skelly.

We started checking it out, and we noticed it had all kind of rooms.

Of course, I was just hoping it had a bathroom.

I know, I know. I could probably just go right here.

But, I'm a little tired of swimming in warm water.

So wrong.

Anyway, as I was checking out one of the rooms, all of a sudden, I heard Steve yelling.

"Dude, come see this!!!"

I swam over to Steve, and it was a **CHEST!**

"Whoa!"

"I bet it's got like treasure in it and stuff," Steve said. "Let's open it,"

"But what if it's like booby trapped or something?" I said. "Or what if we open it, and then we're CURSED to live as the undead for all eternity?"

"Dude, I think you've been watching too many movies."

"I don't know man, this is how it always starts."

"Hey, did you ever think, that maybe there's some brain coral in there?"

You know, Steve had a good point.

"OK, open it."

So we both opened the chest.

CREEAAAAKKK!

"Whoa, it's a **HAT!**"

"Actually," Steve said, putting the hat on, "it's a pirate's hat! ARRRRGGGHHH!!!"

Oh, brother.

Suddenly, a large shadow swam by outside.

"Uh...What was that?"

"What was what?" Steve asked, trying to walk around like a pirate with a wooden leg. "ARRRRGGGHHH!!!

Then the large **SHADOW** passed by again.

"THAT! DID YOU SEE IT?!!!"

"See what?"

Then, all of a sudden Steve turned **WHITER** than I had ever seen him.

Next thing I know, he started pointing behind me.

"Awww man, really?!!!"

Then, I slowly turned around.

"WHAT THE WHAT'N WHAT IS THAT?!!!!!"

There was a giant, monstrous **EYEBALL** looking at us from outside.

Suddenly...

BBBOOOOOMMMM!!!!

"AAAAAAAHHHHHHH!!!!!"

The thing started banging against the ship!

BBBOOOOOMMMM!!!!
BBBOOOOOMMMM!!!!

"AAAAAAAHHHHHHH!!!!!"

"What is that thing?!!!"

"I don't know!" Steve yelled, "But I think he's gonna eat us!"

BBBOOOOOMMMM!!!!
BBBOOOOOMMMM!!!!

"AAAAAAAHHHHHHH!!!!!"

Me and Steve just curled up in a ball in the corner.

"Dude, feed him one of your arms or legs or something," Steve said, "Maybe he'll go away!"

"WHAT?!!!! No way man. You do it. Maybe he's a man-eater."

BBBOOOOOMMMM!!!!
BBBOOOOOMMMM!!!!

"AAAAAAAHHHHHH!!!!!"

"I think he just wants his hat back," a voice said.

"Dude, I'm so scared, I'm hearing things," I said.

"Me, too. It sounded like someone said the thing wants it's hat back."

"I did say that," the voice said again.

"AAAAAAAHHHHHHH!!!!!"

Then I saw a **HAND** come over and take the hat off of Steve's head.

"AAAAAAAHHHHHHH!!!!!"

Then we heard the voice say, "Here you go my little wubbly bubbly. Did those two take your hat? Don't you worry, I got your hat right here. Good boy!"

What the what?

Then me and Steve got up from cowering in the fetal position.

"What is that?" Steve whispered to me, as we both looked at the seaweed covered Zombie standing in front of us.

"Why are you asking me?" I whispered back.

"Who's a good boy? Who's a good boy? **WHO'S A GOOD BOY?**" the thing said to the giant, monstrous eyeball thing outside.

"He kinda looks like you, dude," Steve whispered.

I should've been insulted, but I was kinda too scared to do anything but make bubbles.

"Go talk to him," Steve whispered.

"Alright, alright," I told him, a little annoyed that he was rushing me.

"Excuse me, Mr. green thing, dude, uh... my name is Zombie and I come from Minecraft."

Then the green seaweed covered Zombie guy swam over to me and Steve.

"AAAAAAAHHHHHH!!!!!"

"**DON'T BE AFRAID**. My name is Garth."

Yeah, with a name like Garth, there's no way I was going to be afraid of that guy.

"What are you?" I asked him.

"I'm a Zombie like you. Except I was born **UNDER WATER**"

Me and Steve looked at each and said, "Whoa."

"It's kind of weird to see an Overworld Zombie around these parts," Garth said to me. "They don't normally last very long down here."

Then Steve jumped in, "Hey, what was that thing outside?"

"Oh, you mean my pet **SHARK**, Bubbles? Ah don't mind him. He just gets a little upset when people take his hat."

"Seriously?!!!"

"Oh, and he probably wanted to EAT you Zombie. Overworld Zombies are like a treat around here."

"What?!!!"

"Yes. I told you, Zombies from your world don't last very long down here."

Then Steve gave me the "I told you so look" again.

"Whatevers, man."

"So what are you doing so far away from home?" Garth asked us.

"Well, we're looking for the Lost Ocean Temple of Atlantis," I said.

"Glenda the witch told us we can find some brain coral there."

Then Garth looked really **SURPRISED**.

"Hey, do you know where it is? Glenda said the entrance would come out during the full moon. And we only have a few more hours until the moon is gone."

"Yeah, I know where it is," Garth said, as he started acting **WEIRD**.

"Garth, please show us where it is! We only have a few more hours till the full moon is gone. And if I don't get the brain coral, I'm going to fade from society, become a criminal, and then end up working as a janitor at my school!"

Garth looked at us...confused.

"Uh...Don't mind him, he's been under water a little too long," Steve said. "But seriously, can you help us?

"Yes, I better show you where it is," Garth said. "I'm afraid if I don't go with you, you'll both end up as SHARK FOOD."

"Uh...thanks Garth."

Gulp! I think.

☀ SUNDAY, ☀
EVEN MORE LATER...

After swimming for a while, we finally made it to a huge underwater rock.

"This is it," Garth said. "The Lost Ocean Temple gate is right here."

"What gives?" Steve asked. "It just looks like a GIANT ROCK."

Then suddenly, the clouds parted, and the moon rays lit up the water.

Suddenly the giant rock changed right before our eyes.

Next thing we know a giant gate appeared made out of pearls and diamonds.

"Whoa!"

"Good luck with your quest, gentlemen," Garth said acting all SQUIRRELY.

"You're not coming with us?" Steve said. "We could really use somebody like you on our team."

"Well, I would but..." Then Garth stopped talking and gave us a weird look.

"What aren't you telling us, dude?" I asked him suspiciously.

"Alright! I'll tell you!" Garth blurted. "I escaped okay! I **ESCAPED** from the Lost Ocean Temple of Atlantis!"

Steve and I gave each other a look.

"Escaped from what?" Steve asked him.

"Don't go in there!" Garth kept blurting. "You'll never come back out alive! Forget the brain coral. Be a janitor! At least you'll survive. But don't ever go in there!"

Gulp!

"Dude, honestly, this guy is giving me the creeps," I whispered to Steve. "I mean, I would rather be a live janitor than a dead Zombie."

"But you are a dead Zombie," Steve said.

"Urrggghh! You know what I mean."

"You sure you want to **GIVE UP**?" Steve asked me. "I mean, being left back is really not that bad. Like, you'll probably lose all your friends, kids will point at you and make fun at you in the hallways, and parents will use you as a bedtime story to scare their kids. But at least you'll become a legend, like Larry Lardbottom."

"Well, when you put it that way..."

"I thought so," Steve said as he puffed out his ruffles.

"Sorry Garth, we're going in, because we never give up," Steve said. "Not when there's too much at stake."

"Well, since I can't talk you out of it, then I guess I have to warn you. Be very careful not to be seen. All of the mobs in the Ocean Temple are under the **KING'S SPELL**. And they will attack anyone who does not serve the King's orders."

"King? What king?"

"King Coral," Garth said with a scared look on his face. "King Coral is the meanest king that has ever reigned over the seven seas...and under it."

Of course, he is.

"Yes, and if you still want the brain coral, the only place to find it is on **KING CORAL'S CROWN**. He uses the brain coral to amplify his mind control powers."

Mind control powers. Figures.

"I escaped because King Coral made the entire kingdom his slaves, so that they could mine for more brain coral. He was obsessed with looking for the motherload of all the brain coral. It was even said that if he found it, he will be able to control the minds of all the mobs in the ocean...and ultimately the entire Overworld."

Then me and Steve looked at each other.

"DUN, DUN, DUUUNNNNNN!"

Then we burst out laughing.

"Yeah, whatevers man," Steve said, puffing out his chest. "We eat **DANGER** for breakfast."

"Yeah...Breakfast, he..he..." I said as my chest sank down to my feet.

"Well, good luck to you both," Garth said, looking really ashamed he wasn't coming with us.

"Yeah...thanks," I said, getting the feeling that maybe being a janitor wasn't such a bad idea.

"Well, let's do this," Steve said, excited as a bunny rabbit at a carrot convention.

"I really hate you, you know that?"

Then Steve smiled and gave me a big **THUMBS UP**.

Then we both walked through the gates to the Lost Ocean Temple of Atlantis.

* SUNDAY, *
LIKE, MUCH,
MUCH LATER...

When we got through the gate portal to the Lost Ocean Temple, there wasn't anybody around.

"I guess they don't get a lot of **VISITORS**," I said. "So, where's the ocean temple?"

Then Steve pointed up.

Then as me and Steve looked up, there it was. The biggest, most amazing Temple we had ever seen.

"Whoa! That's awesome!" Steve and I both said at the same time.

It was blue, like the water, but it shimmered like if was made out of **DIAMONDS**.

As we swam closer, for some reason, there was nobody around.

"Where is everybody?" I asked him.

"Look over there," Steve said pointing to the giant caves outside the temple.

There was **SMOKE** coming from the caves, like if somebody was mining for something.

"Let's go see what's going on," Steve said.

So Steve and I swam over to one of the caves, and snuck in.

As we swam deeper and deeper in the caves, the noise started getting louder and louder, and the water started getting hotter and hotter.

Then, we reached a giant underwater **CAVERN**.

"Dude, check that out," Steve said.

Inside the giant underwater cavern it looked like thousands of mobs were mining for something.

"This must be where they're **MINING** for the brain coral." Steve said.

"Oh, man. Do you think if he finds it, he's going to take over the world?" I asked him.

"What do you think?"

"Yeah, dumb question."

"This is you chance to get some brain coral," Steve said.

"You mean I have to go down there? They're going to see me for sure."

"I got an idea," Steve said. Then he started collecting some SEAWEED from the cave, and anything else he could find.

Then he started putting it on me.

"There it is." Steve said proudly. "Perfect."

Steve took a picture with his underwater camera, and then he showed me.

"Dude, I look like a dufus." I said.

"Yeah, but after you get that brain coral, you'll be a "I just aced my math final, dufus."

Yeah, he had a point.

Well, I needed to go down to the mine, act like a mind-controlled **OCEAN NOOB**, grab some brain coral, and then high tail it out of this place.

Why do I get the feeling its not going to be as easy as it sounds?

Well, here goes nothing.

✳ SUNDAY – ✳
I THINK YOU
GET THE PICTURE...

"Urrrgh. I'm a slave. I am boring.
I like eating boogers. King Coral is
awesome."

I said whatever I could to convince
the guards that I was LEGIT.

I wasn't sure if my costume was
enough to convince them that I was an
underwater mob enslaved by the mind
control powers of tyrannical ruler.

But to be honest, pretending to be
enslaved is not that hard.

That's what having parents is all about.

And yep, they had guards.

They were these huge **GUARDIANS**, and they were all keeping their eye on things.

Get it...keeping an eye on things...tee, hee.

I was kinda wondering why they needed guards, since everybody was under King Coral's mind control.

But I guess if he had to go number two, he'd probably need a backup team to keep an eye on things.

I mean like, when I go number two, I'm so out of it, I fall **ASLEEP** on the toilet sometimes.

One time I fell asleep on the toilet, and when I woke up, my face was all wet.

Don't ask.

I still try not to think about it.

"Urgh, I'm a **SLAVE**. Look at me. I'm boring...Urgh."

It looked like it was working.

The guards didn't even look twice at me.

And I could see my **PRIZE** right in front of me.

There was huge mountain of brain coral at the end of the cave. It's where everybody was dumping the brain coral they found.

All I had to do was go over there, grab a piece, and then get back to Steve.

And I had the perfect place to hide it too.

It's where I hide all the stuff that they say I can't bring to school.

That's right, in between my butt cheeks.

I can hide all kind of things in there.

Things like my cell phone. Or my booger snacks. Or my fidget cube.

Hey, a kid's gotta have something to distract himself most of the day, you know.

And my fidget cube works great...I mean, after you get used to the **SMELL**.

I do get some strange looks from the other kids when I pull it out, though.

Especially in the cafeteria.

After I grabbed a piece of brain coral, I hid it away in my butt cheeks, really good.

It did have some sharp edges, though.

Kinda felt like I sat on a
PORCUPINE.

But when I tried to get back the way
I came, all of a sudden, the guards
rotated, and a huge guardian blocked
my way.

He even started looking at me funny,
so I started walking the other way.

So now, the only other way out was
through the main cave entrance.

But I couldn't go that way, because it
looked like everybody that left through
the main entrance had to go through
a really thorough **SECURITY
CHECK.**

I mean like, they looked in your pockets, they looked in your clothes, and they even looked in your mouth.

They even stuck their fingers in places that hands should never go...

...Like their noses.

NASTY.

So, I had to find another way out.

"There he is! Get him!" All the guards yelled.

Oh man! The jig is up!

I thought I was caught for sure.

But then they swam past me and swam toward Steve.

Oh boy.

But, at least it gave me the opportunity to **ESCAPE.**

As soon as all the guards started chasing after Steve, I inched my way closer and closer to the main entrance.

And then, just when I was about to make it out...

"Where do you think you're going?" A giant Elder Guardian said, as he looked me over with his one eye.

"Urgh. I am a slave and I like to do homework. Urgh."

Then, the Elder guardian looked me over, and scanned me with his big eyeball.

Talk about awkward.

"Hey! What's that in your **BACK POCKET**?" the elder guardian asked me.

"Urgh. I am a slave and I like to do my taxes...and listen to old people music? Urgh."

"Hand it over, right now."

Suddenly, I got really nervous and dropped the brain coral that I was hiding.

But as soon as I bent down to pick it up, the rest of my seaweed costume fell off.

"Here's another one! **GET HIM!**"

Then the guards all surrounded me and scanned me with their big eyes.

I started feeling dizzy.

Until suddenly... everything went black.

M✳NDAY
...FINALLY! ✳

"Ooohhh, my head," I said, trying to stand up.

"Hey man, give it a minute. The **DIZZINESS** will go way," I heard Steve say.

"What?!! They got you too?"

"Yeah man, they zapped me with their eyebeams and knocked me right out."

"Where are we?"

"Where do you think?"

"Let me guess...A nasty old dungeon, with only one way out?"

"Yep."

"And in a few minutes, the evil villain is going to come in and tell us his whole plan of world **DOMINATION?**"

"Yep."

Figures.

I hadn't even finished my thought, when the door to the dungeon creaked open.

Next thing I know, the weirdest squid faced looking guy

with a huge brain floated in, with two guardians at his side.

"Now, you must be Zombie, and you must be Steve...and I know you are here to **STEAL** my brain coral," Squidface said.

"And let me guess," Steve said. "You must be King Coral, and you're using your big brain hat to read our minds, and figure out what we are thinking?"

"Hey, how did you know that?" the king blurted.

"And you are going to tell us your **DIABOLICAL** plan to take over the ocean, right?" I said.

"Hey, who told you?"

"And then after that, you are going to try to take over the entire overworld, right? Steve said.

"Hey, you're spoiling my speech!" the king said, getting all ANNOYED and sweaty.

Then me and Steve just burst out laughing.

"Well, I bet you didn't know about the shark," King Coral said, with a creepy smile.

"Let me guess," Steve said, "There's a giant shark waiting to eat my friend Zombie over there, and you're going to feed my friend to him, in a giant arena while everybody watches, right?"

"Actually, I was just going to tell you that you had a **CHOICE** between shark or tuna for lunch, but I like your idea even better," King Coral said.

Gulp!

"Zombie, you can be our main event tonight," the King continued. "Oh how **DELICIOUS**, you will be after you are torn into little bite size morsels."

What the what?!!!

"Hey, what about me?!!!" Steve said.

"I can use a person like you Steve. With a little mental conditioning, you will be the **PERFECT SPY** to gain the trust of everyone in the Overworld. You will do my bidding, so that taking over the overworld will be a piece of cake."

Yup...here it comes.

"MUAHAHAHAHAHAHAHA!"

"MUAHAHAHAHAHAHAHA!"

"MUAHAHAHAHAHAHAHA!"

Then they left.

"I really **HATE** you, you know that?" I said to Steve.

Then he gave me a weak smile and a thumbs up.

M✱NDAY
...YEAH, YOU✱ GUESSED IT...LATER...

As the guards walked me into the giant under water arena, all I could see all around me were the bones of all the different **VICTIMS** before me.

There were squid bones, turtle bones, dolphin bones...

They even had bones from of a big square sponge, and a really fat starfish.

All I can say is that I was so scared, I cracked my cell phone.

And as I looked up, all I could see were hundreds of underwater mobs waiting to be entertained.

King Coral was there, sitting on is throne.

And Steve was next to him.

Though I could tell from Steve's blank expression that King Coral had already started working his mind **CONTROL MAGIC** on him.

"RRRRAAAWWWRRRRRR!!!!"

WHAT THE WHAT WAS THAT?!!!

The noise came from behind a giant door, that had a giant chain, and had giant bite marks on it.

Then the crowd started
CHEERING...

"YEAH! BRING HIM OUT! TEAR THE ZOMBIE TO SHREDS! AND LET'S EAT WHAT'S LEFT OVER!

Suddenly, the water started getting really warm around me again.

The guards led me to the middle of the arena, and they took off my shackles.

Then suddenly, they opened the giant door.

"RRRRAAAWWWRRRRRR!!!!"

Then the biggest, scariest, ugliest and meanest looking shark came out.

They had the giant monster chained, so he couldn't get away until they were nice and ready.

By that point, whatever I had for my last meal just exited my body and floated past my face.

Then King Coral made an **ANNOUNCEMENT**.

"Zombie, we found this beautiful specimen swimming outside of the temple looking for food. It was drawn to the smell of rotten flesh. So we brought him in especially for you..."

"So, let the games begin!"

Then they released the giant beast and he swam straight for his Zombie snack.

The crowd went wild.

YEAAAAHHHHH!!!!

Oh man, this is it!

As the giant **EATING MACHINE** swam closer toward me, I tried to move, but I was frozen with fear.

And as he got closer and closer, my whole life flashed before my eyes.

I looked up at Steve for some help, but he was totally out of it.

This is it. This is the end. I thought.

So, I just closed my eyes, and waited for the inevitable.

I knew in any minute I would be **SHARK CHOW.**

Oh man, this is gonna really hurt, I thought.

Suddenly, I felt something land on my head.

What the what?

I reached over and felt it, and it was...a hat?

And then what looked like a giant fork hit the ground.

Thump!

Thanks, whoever threw it, I thought. Now when he eats me, at least he'll have some manners.

So I took off the hat and held it to my chest in honor of all the brave souls that came before me.

Goodbye cruel world...

Suddenly, the giant shark **STOPPED** in his tracks.

Huh?!!!!

And then, as I moved my arm, with the hat in my hand, the shark just followed it.

"What the...?"

"RRRRHRRREWW?"

Wait! No way! This couldn't be...?

"Bubbles?"

"RRRRHRRREWW!"

It is!

"Who's a good boy? Who's a good boy? **WHO'S A GOOD BOY?**"

Then I put the hat on Bubble's head, and he turned sideways so I could scratch his belly.

Then that must mean...

As I looked up, I could see a green looking guy waving at me from the stands.

"Garth!"

Then he started waving his arms and making gestures.

It looked he was telling me to pick up the giant fork.

So I picked it up, jumped on Bubbles and swam for King Coral!

Then the whole arena **ERUPTED** with yelling and screaming, and mobs were running all over the place.

"AAAAAHHHHHHH!!!!"

I didn't care, because I was going to save my friend and then get the hey out of there.

Then, as I got closer, King Coral said something to Steve, and then backed away.

It didn't matter because all I cared about was getting my friend back.

As I made it to the throne room, I jumped off Bubbles, made it over to Steve and grabbed his big square arm.

"**COME ON MAN**, let's get out of here!"

And I was totally not ready for what came next...

M✺NDAY
...YOU WOULDN'T BELIEVE WHAT HAPPENED...

POWWWWWW!!!!

Steve **CLOCKED** me so hard, it almost knocked my head clean off.

"Dude, what gives man!"

"I serve King Coral," Steve said, in a robot voice. "He is my master now."

"You can't help him now," King Coral laughed. "He is now totally under my **CONTROL**!"

"MUAHAHAHAHA!"

Then Steve came back for another attack.

"Steve, come on man. You're better than this. Don't let him get to you dude!"

Steve pulled back for another **SWING.**

I got out of the way just in time.

BOOOOMMMMM!!!

Steve punched so hard, it exploded the giant pillar next to King Coral's throne.

Man, I knew punching trees made you strong, but not that strong.

Then Steve **CORNERED** me, so I couldn't escape.

"This is the end for you, Zombie," Kind Coral kept taunting. "There's no escape for you now!"

"MUAHAHAHAHA!"

Urrrggh. So cliché.

I could hear Garth yelling something from far away.

"Use the Trident!"

"Use the Trident!"

And when I turned to look at Garth, he was making signs that I should use the GIANT FORK.

Oh man, what was I going to do?

I couldn't hit my best friend with the giant fork.

But I knew Steve's next punch was going to like, totally disintegrate me.

But what was I going to do?

Everything after that, just shifted into slow motion.

Steve pulled back really far for
another punch.

Right then, I grabbed the Trident and
pulled it up in
front of me
to deflect the
attack.

Then
suddenly...

ZZZZAAAAAAAPPPPP!!!!!
BOOOOOOOMM!!!

Steve hit the Trident full force,
and the explosion blew him back like
twenty feet.

I ran over to him, to make sure he was okay.

But Steve got up again, ready for another attack.

"Ha, ha! He's not going to stop until you are **DESTROYED**!" King Coral kept taunting me.

But this time, I didn't have the heart to fight back.

Steve pulled back his arm once more for one final punch.

And I just dropped the Trident, opened my arms, to face my fate.

Then as Steve's arm slowly moved
through the air...Suddenly, it turned up.

Then Steve
smiled at me
and gave me a
thumbs up.

M✱NDAY
...YUP, THERE'S MORE...

"No, this cannot be!" King Coral yelled.

"It's over King Coral, time to hang up the crown," I told him.

"You will just have to become my **MINION** as well!" King Coral said.

Then he put up his tentacles and started pointing them at me.

I started feeling tingly, and weird.

And then suddenly...

PFFFFT!

"Oh, excuse me...tee, hee."

"What is going on? Why is this not working?!!!" King Coral blurted, as he kept pointing his tentacles at me.

"I don't know, but I know what does work!" I yelled.

Then I took the **TRIDENT** and pulled it over my head.

Steve pulled his arm back and then...

ZZZZAAAAAAAPPPPP!!!!!
BOOOOOOOMM!!!

The force from Steve's punch hitting the Trident totally blew us all like twenty feet.

But more importantly, it **SMASHED** King Coral's brain coral crown into like a million pieces.

"My crown!!! Noooooooooo!!!!!

Then two huge Elder Guardians entered the throne room with Garth in hand.

"I'll get you for this! Guards! Grab them!" King Coral yelled.

Then the Elder Guardians rushed toward me and Steve.

"Take them and throw them in the bottomless pit!" King Coral yelled.

But then the guards walked right past us and grabbed King Coral by the tentacles.

"What?!!! What are you doing?!!!! **STOP!**"

Then one of the Elder Guardian walked over to Garth.

"Sir, what would you like us to do with him?" He asked Garth.

"You heard his orders, take him to the bottomless pit." Garth said.

"Yes, sir!!!!" The guards all yelled.

"I'll get you for this! I'll get my revenge! You'll see! I'll be back!" King Coral kept yelling.

Then Steve and I both looked at each other.

"DUN, DUN, DUNNNNN!"

Then we burst out laughing.

"Hey, Garth, what's this *Sir* stuff?" I asked him.

"Well, I was **PRINCE** of the Lost Ocean Temple of Atlantis before King Coral took over. And now that the spell is finally broken, my people are free, and I can lead them again." Garth said. "And it's all thanks to both of you, Zombie and Steve. How can we ever repay you?"

"Well, a little brain coral would be nice," I said.

"Unfortunately, we're going to have to **DESTROY** all the brain coral. We've got to make sure it never lands in the wrong hands again," Garth said. "But, how about a ride back home?"

"Sounds great."

Then me, Steve and Garth jumped on Bubbles, and got the hey out of there.

TUESDAY

Well, we finally made it back to land, and back to our villages.

And I was so happy to be back.

That is until I **REALIZED**...

Today's my math final! Urrrrrggghhh!

And I don't have any brain coral potion to make me smarter.

And I haven't studied either.

What do you mean why didn't I study?

Well besides having a brain the size of a pea, I had no time, you know.

I was **TOO BUSY** fighting Zombie eating sharks, hiding from humongous guardians and battling an insane Squid with serious ego issues.

And yeah, I know if I don't pass this math final, I'm going to be left back, fade from society, and become a janitor, blah, blah, blah.

But, you know what? All I can do, is do my best... so that's what I'm going to do.

Well, here goes nothing...

 TUESDAY,
LATER...

Guess what?

I **FAILED** my math test.

Yep...I'm toast.

So, after school I went to the principal's office to get an earful.

And to pick up my janitor's job application.

When I got there, the secretary said that the Principal was waiting for me in his office.

Then, I started to **FEEL SICK** again.

GRRRRRRRRRRR!

The secretary gave me a disgusted look as she put on her raincoat.

Smart move.

When I got to the door of the Principal's office, I felt like I was about to explode.

And as the door opened, Larry Lardbottom the janitor, was there cleaning his office.

"Hey, Larry. Uh...Where's Creeper Principal Brown?"

"Oh, Principal Brown doesn't work here anymore," Larry said, sitting on Principal Brown's desk. "His doctor said something about the stress being too much for him."

"Seriously?!!!!"

But I could tell Larry was right.

There were still GREEN CHUNKS sliding down the walls.

Whose idea was it to make a creeper the Principal, I don't know.

But something tells me they really didn't think that one through.

But I wasn't sure if I should celebrate, or hurl.

I mean, who knows? The next Principal might be like ten times **WORSE** than Principal Brown.

"So, how are you doing, Zombie?" Larry asked me.

"Uh...I'm good. I failed my math final though."

"Yeah, I heard. Ms. Bones told me."

What's Ms. Bones doing talking to the janitor? I thought. Especially about my personal life.

Adults...So weird.

"So did you do your best?"

"Man, I sure did. But no matter how much I tried, I couldn't remember anything. It's a Zombie pea brain thing, you know."

"Why didn't just use a **MATH APP**? There's a really good one called Math for Dummies," Larry said.

"Yeah, well, you wouldn't understand."

"Try me," Larry said, acting all mature and stuff.

"Well, I used a math app once, and I got a perfect score on my math test. Not only that, but it was the first time that math was really fun for me."

"Really?"

"Yeah, I actually liked doing the problems. It kinda felt like I was playing a video game or something. I was even kinda sad when the test was over."

"So, using the app made math a **LOT OF FUN** for you?"

"Mmmm...Hmmm."

"And it was so much fun, that you were sad when it was over?"

""Mmmm...Hmmm."

"And if it was up to you, you would do as much math you could, because it's so much fun, like playing a video game?

"Yeah!"

Why Larry asking me so much
questions, I didn't know. But then
I started feeling sick again when
I thought about meeting the new
Principal.

"So, where's the new **PRINCIPAL?**"
I asked him.

"You're looking at him," Larry said.

"What?!!!!!"

"Yep, I was just hired today. It's my
first day."

"But, you're like a janitor, and you
dropped out of society, and you're like
a criminal, and..."

Larry just stood there looking at me...
Confused.

"I mean, how?!!!"

"Well, the school board contacted all
the kids that **GRADUATED** and
became very successful in life. And
they asked them to vote on who they
would think would make the best
principal..."

"Yeah, so."

"Well, for some reason my name came
up. And when they all took a final
vote, I got the job."

"Seriously? But, why?

"Well, everybody said that when they
were all stressed out in school, and

felt like nobody could help them, I kinda stepped in and encouraged them to just do their best. They said they just need somebody to tell them that if they did good in school, it was great. But if not, that was fine too."

"Really?"

"Yeah. They said they just needed somebody to tell them it was okay to just be themselves. Because, they could never **FAIL** at that."

"Whoa."

"After that, they weren't so stressed out anymore about tests, and papers, and grades, and homework. Then everything was a lot easier after that."

Wow, Larry reminds me a lot of Steve.

So, cool.

"But, you did fail your test, Zombie,"
Larry said. "So, were going to have to
do something about that."

I started feeling sick again.

GRRRRRRRR!

I could see the secretary outside put
her raincoat back on.

RRRRRRIIIIIPPPPP!

What the what?!!!!

Larry just **RIPPED** my test in half!

"I want you to take your test again, Zombie. Except this time, I want you to use your math app, or a calculator, or whatever else you think you need to do it."

"Seriously?!!!!!"

"Yep. I already told Ms. Bones about it. So she's waiting for you in your class with a makeup test **RIGHT NOW.**"

He didn't have to ask me twice!

So I grabbed my phone, my calculator, my pencils and my booger snacks.

I ran into Ms. Bones class, and by her facial expression, I could tell she wasn't too happy about letting me use my tools to pass the test.

But it didn't really matter.

...Because I was going to do this test **MY WAY!**

WEDNESDAY

Well, I aced my math final today.

Yes!

I even got the **HIGHEST** score out of the entire eighth-grade.

I think it was because of all the extra credit I did...

Or, they probably liked my booger sculpture of Ms. Bones.

Hey, I finished really early, so I had a lot of extra time on my hands.

What's really cool is that our school is totally **DIFFERENT** now.

Instead of worrying about grades, term papers, and homework, now we kinda learn what we want, and how we want to.

We even get to teach some of the classes!

Like, I just started a Video Game Design class at my school.

All we do is design and play video games all day. But the best part is, I get credit for it in school!

Yes!

Skelly is really into **MUSIC**, so he started a band called The Walking Dead 2. Check out his pic.

Slimey is teaching a Life Guard Swimming Class. He even holds contests for the kids with the best belly flops.

And Creepy was going to teach a Parkour class, but we kinda talked him out of it.

Even Steve is getting in on the action.

He started teaching a night class called Tree Punching 101, so now we get a lot of villagers come to our school after work.

He tried teaching a night **MINING** class too, but it didn't go so well.

Ooooooo. So wrong.

You know, I was still wondering why King Coral's mind control powers didn't work on me.

But later, Garth told me it was because Overworld Zombie brains are **TOO SMALL** for the mind control to work on us.

So now, I actually feel really good that I have a pea brain.

I mean, I still tend to forget a lot of things.

But it comes in really handy when I have to do **CHORES**.

"What do you mean Mom? What dishes?"

Tee, hee.

Garth sends his regards by the way.

He and Bubbles are both doing really good.

He even sent a pic.

Anyway, it's time for me to get back to **my VIDEO GAME DESIGN CLASS.**

Today we're designing a new game called Zombie's Vs. Aliens.

Man, it's going to be awesome.

And I totally can't wait to see how it turns out!

THE END